Luring the Alien
Reeling in the Alien Book 2
Alina Riley

Copyright © 2023 by Alina Riley

All rights reserved.

No portion of this book may be reproduced in any form without written permission from the publisher or author, except as permitted by U.S. copyright law.

Chapter 1

Vikul

Flying in a spaceship is boring and stupid. Someone should have invented a better way to travel in space.

I drum my fingers on the dashboard as I stare at the window. Maybe I should get a nap. This spaceship drives itself anyway, so it isn't like I have to sit around.

I stand and stretch my arms. I've done my job well already, but being in this part of the universe...

How is this possible? There won't be a single portal around here? For another day?

I resist the urge to punch the dashboard. It won't hurt the stupid portal anyway, and I'm not going to pay to repair my own spaceship.

While the spaceship is floating here in the middle of nowhere, I scroll the map on the screen of the dashboard. There are planets around, but none of them look interesting.

There is this tiny little planet called Earth where there should be beings there I can communicate with.

Hm... A mostly blue planet with some green.

I scroll down to read the description of it. It seems to be a fine planet for me to spend some time on. I've just finished looking for rare gems on nearby planets, so it will be great to be on a planet...

Wait... Under the description box and the details about gaseous components, it said, no landing there and no communicating with the beings there unless I have authorization.

I scoff and roll my eyes at that. Who even follows that? And who will be here to catch me anyway?

I'm not a fool. There are humans on other planets, so there has to be someone bringing them there.

The more I think about the warning for landing on Earth, the more I want to have a look. It's just a peek anyway. It isn't like the humans will be able to see me.

I tap the buttons and steer my spaceship to Earth. Here I go. No one gets to stop me!

There is a thick layer of clouds and moisture in the atmosphere of Earth. I stare at the boring white and gray, stifling a yawn. Maybe this is just a boring planet. Humans can't be that interesting anyway. I've seen some already.

They are pretty smart and with pale skin. I glance at my hand. Almost completely different from my purple skin.

Hmm... The clouds slowly clear and I'm staring at a large piece of blue. There is nothing other than the blue. The information chart said there should be humans or, at least, some buildings.

I tap on the screen and check again. So... the blue is the ocean and humans don't build things on top of oceans.

Fine, I will go and search for somewhere I can see humans. It can't be that hard. I will just move the ship to one side.

There they are. There is a light brown patch next to the ocean. I tap for the screen to zoom in. There are humans there and all of them seem to be lying around on the pale brown ground.

What are they doing there?

I squint at them, tapping to catch different angles. Looks like all of those are humans. There are different skin colors, but none of them looks like another species. Is that the reason I shouldn't land there?

If I walk into that place, maybe everyone will stare at me.

I fold my arms and stare at the screen. Maybe I won't land there. But I'm still going to be here in the air, watching these humans walking around in black glasses. That's weird.

I check the information sheet again. perspective can be weird when I'm up so high. The document said that the place is called a beach. It is formed by the sedimentation of sand. Ah, then I understand. The sand here looks to be a different color from the ones I've seen. Anyway...

Wait...

I scroll the map and go back to what I glanced at. There is a woman sitting under a tree in a cute two-piece that barely covers her boobs and her groin. I scratch my head and rub my ear. There are a lot of women dressing like that on the beach, but somehow, I feel the need to stare at this one.

She has beautiful brown hair, but she doesn't look relaxed like the other humans. There's no way she can see me, right?

I suppose staring at a woman like this isn't very comfortable, but she doesn't know.

I roll my eyes. I feel like a creep, but something in me screams at how I need her in my life.

She's looking at her phone in her hand. Is she waiting for someone?

There is a fire in my stomach for some reason. She better not be waiting for a male. I clench my fist even though I don't even know who she is and have never seen her before.

She's still looking around. She is sitting on a small beach mat with watermelons on it. The mat is too small for two humans, even though they are smaller than troculs.

I suck in a breath. I'm not supposed to talk to or meet a human that's on Earth, but...

The urge inside me grows and the rule-follower in me, who already barely exists, is fading. I want her and I will figure out the reason later.

Chapter 2

Galene

I take a deep breath when my heart is pounding in my chest. I'm supposed to be spending my vacation days here on a beach — relaxed. But I can't stop myself from looking around at other people.

I don't have to care about them, but...

I put my phone to the side and push my finger into the warm sand. Today is a great day with a clear blue sky and gentle wind. I don't have to worry about others looking at me; they probably aren't looking at me anyway. When there is the sea and the amazing view out there, who is going to look at me?

That's what I should think and feel, but I can't help feeling that everyone is staring at me. I must look dumb in a bikini. I don't look that good after all.

I stare at my stomach, which doesn't look slim enough. I pinch it and sigh. Maybe I'm the only one who cares about this. Or maybe I should stay in a T-shirt and shorts. Those are also beach wear and no one will bat an eye if I do that. Somehow, I chose to wear the bikini...

This is supposed to be the time for me to snap out of my self-consciousness and enjoy my day. Dammit!

I clench a fist into the fine sand, watching them slide back to the ground. I even chose to be on a beach far away from my hometown so I won't run into anyone i know.

But...

I grab a can of sparkling water from the cooler, pop it, and take a sip. The cool liquid runs down my throat but doesn't quench the ups and downs inside me.

I don't want to sit here on the beach, but if I stand and walk around, I'd be attracting attention.

But I shouldn't care about what others think and I should be enjoying the sea, which is right in front of me!

There are people walking in front of me and kids running around, none of them are looking at me, yet... It still feels like someone is watching me. Am I too anxious? Imagining things?

I down the sparkling water and lie on the mat instead. I'm going to enjoy the day. So much for worrying about others. I'm going to snap out of that in no time. Maybe I don't look perfect. I'm still pretty good the way I am.

The sound of the waves kissing the shoreline and the seagulls calms me. When the wind blows against the trees, it is fine music that I don't get in my busy day-to-day life. This is going to be a great vacation.

I shudder when it feels like something hits me, but when I open my eyes, there's no one near me. It can't be someone tossing sand onto me, right? That'll be beyond silly.

A surge of sleepiness rushes into me. I stifle a yawn, but my limbs grow tired quicker than I imagined. So strange. Maybe the drive to get here exhausted me more than I imagined.

I... will... just... take—

I fall back and land on something soft. It must be the beach mat. Darkness surrounds me. My eyelids and the sunglasses are working well together, so well that I can't even feel the power of the sun. I take a breath, letting myself slide into a slumber...

Chapter 3

Galene

I open my eyes to see... I thought I'd been under a palm tree, but I'm not there now. Above me is a pale gray ceiling.

Hmm...

There is a numb pain in my head. Is that from the nap? Sometimes, if I take a long nap, my head hurts. But I'm not even on the beach. What the hell?

I pat my sides. There isn't a hint of sand, but fabric, as if I'm on a bed.

Why am I on a bed?

Did I get a heatstroke and some medics put me else-where?

I sit up on the bed to stare at a map on the wall across the bed. I squint at that. It doesn't look like a map of places I know. To be precise, it doesn't look like a map of places on Earth. But I suppose there can be small countries here that I'm not familiar with.

I shake my head. Why would someone put a map of a far-away place on the wall here? It doesn't make any sense.

No one is inside the room, though. There is no tube and nothing on me to monitor my vitals. Maybe I'm not in a first-aid place. But...

I check out myself. I'm still in my bikini and I look intact. This room is cool and at a nice temperature for a nap, but I'm not in that mood anymore. Something is very wrong. Say...

Where's my cooler and my phone?

I get off the bed. "Hello? Is someone here?"

My voice echoes in the room with no one coming over. Did I get kidnapped? But... Kidnapped off a busy beach?

There is a desk to the side of the room, and it seems like someone's bedroom. I take a step back and check out the bed. It is a lot larger than the bed I used to sleep on. Definitely intended for more than one person and not the kind of bed hospitals and caring facilities would offer.

I go to the door when it slides open.

I jump a step back when there seems to be someone on the other side.

"Oh, you woke up."

It's a man... wait, no...

I tilt my head to the side at this purple being in front of me. He is probably seven feet tall, very muscular, half-naked... There are tattoos around his chest and on his shoulders. More importantly, he is purple.

Am I having a heat stroke and seeing things? Humans aren't purple. Even when humans are bruised, they don't look this purple.

He is watching me with a grin. Maybe he is enjoying the attention.

I scowl. "Who are you? Why am I here?"

"Hello, I'm Vikul. Nice to meet you." He keeps that annoying grin, as if he is proud of getting me here in this weird room.

"Why am I here? Did you kidnap me? Also, why are you purple?"

"Oh, kidnap. I suppose you can say that. I saw you on the beach." He leans closer to me. He is taller than me, but the way he looks at me...

I shiver and resist the urge to take a step back. What is he planning to do?

He says, "I had the urge to get you here with me, so this is how it is now."

What the actual fuck?

"Hell no! I'm leaving now!" I brace myself and head to the door, which he is blocking with his huge body. Maybe I should be more concerned about how I'm here with a hulky male for no good reason, but if I show him I'm nervous, maybe he'll take that as a hint to do whatever he wants to.

"Well, where are you going?" He takes a step to the side and lets me get out of the door.

Outside...

Where am I?

It's a corridor, and there are two sides for me to pick from. The ceiling is high and the corridors are wide, but... Something doesn't feel right.

There is a humming sound from the air-conditioner or some kind of machinery. The air is dry and cool. This place...

I turn around to see him leaning on the door with a teasing smirk.

He says, "Feel free to walk around. We'll be here for a while anyway."

"No, I'm going home."

He shrugs. "Except you are on my spaceship now, so you aren't going anywhere."

Spaceship?

My heart skips a beat as I eye him up and down again. Um... So...

I take a step back. "You're an alien."

He lifts his brows. "I suppose so. I've heard that's what humans on Earth call us; the beings that live on other planets."

There is no fucking way this is real. He's an alien? This isn't some kind of prank, right?

If he's an alien, it would explain why he's purple. I can accept that there are purple beings living somewhere in space, but... dammit! Of all people, this had to happen to me?

I point at him with my finger shaking. "You are an alien and you kidnapped me."

"Yes, I know humans are smart."

I suck in a breath as I decide whether I should be scared of him or not. He is an alien... I've never seen an alien before. I didn't even know that they exist.

He huffs and rolls his eyes. "What's wrong with you? You are acting as if you have never seen an alien before."

I burst out laughing, even though I probably shouldn't. "Duh?"

"Really?" He scowls. "No way. You must be joking."

"No, I'm not. I've never met an alien before and since you don't seem to be hurting me, I'm not sure whether I should be scared about you or what."

He blinks. "No, you don't have to be scared of me. I'm not going to hurt you."

"So..." My heart is racing. I feel tiny in front of him, even though I'm not that tiny. I may not be tall, but in terms of mass, I'm not small. Not huge, but not small either. "What are you going to do to me?"

He spreads his hand to the side. "Tell me you don't think humans are the only intellectual beings that exist."

I shrug. "No clue. Are you intelligent?"

Something about him feels like home. It feels like I've known him for a long time, even though that makes completely no sense at all. I've never met a purple alien in my life and therefore he should feel like a stranger. With his height and muscles, he should be intimidating, but strangely... he isn't that way to me. I'm not even scared enough to stop my jokes.

He groans. "Human, how dare you? I'm intelligent, otherwise, why are we even talking?"

I chuckle. "We can both be not intelligent at all."

He sighs. "What have I gotten myself into...?"

"Well, you kidnapped me here, so I think you're supposed to know."

He doesn't seem like a criminal or someone who is used to kidnapping beings. Otherwise, he would probably lock me up. I don't know whether he can get a ransom for me, though. Imagine telling my family I'm kidnapped by an alien... They'd laugh so hard that their stomachs would hurt.

He smirks and comes closer and closer until he has me backed against the wall. He is fucking huge when I stare at him up close.

My heart races when he leans in. Something about him lights a fire inside me. Something... Something that burns me hot and pulls me to him...

"My cute little human, you look so tasty."

"You want to make me into your dinner?" That doesn't sound interesting. I suppose he can get some meat off me and quite some fat, but... "Your species... eats other beings?"

He lifts my chin. "Galene, I want you. When I saw you, I didn't understand why I wanted to get you here, but now, I do..."

"How did you know my name?"

"Found your cards." He winks as if he is so proud of himself over that.

I suppose... Lust looks the same in his species as humans... I swallow with my throat dry, but with heat inside me.

"What? You want to fuck me?"

He blinks, seemingly not expecting that. "Well, can't say I don't. But only if you want to. I can give you the perfect trocul cock."

I suck in a breath. So... I ran into an alien who kidnapped me and now he offers to fuck me... This is crazy.

My eyes drift to his crouch. He has quite a hard-on. He is standing so close to me that I can feel the heat from his body. "But you kidnapped me."

"We will be perfect together." He looks more serious than I expected. "You will understand soon and I'll make you want to stay."

"And how are you going to achieve that? Hey—!"

I regret my words at once as he swoops me off the floor into his arms. I guess this is the perk that comes with his strong muscles. I've never felt an alien's cock before... This is going to be interesting.

He lifts me bridal style and makes big strides into the room. "Well, you won't regret your stay here. I can promise that."

"Confident in yourself, huh?"

"I knew it from the moment I saw you."

Maybe that's why it felt like someone had been watching me. My heart races when he puts me on his bed again. He hovers over me with an intense gaze that burns.

I reach for his trousers. "I don't understand why you brought me here, but you better deliver."

He growls and takes off my bikini. "Not a problem."

Chapter 4

Vikul

I put Galene on my bed. This time, she knows she is here with me and I can't wait.

Maybe it is wrong to lust over a female who I've just met. But when I know that she is my mate, it is hard to resist myself. I want to claim her already. She makes my cock twitch and I get so hard that it hurts.

I take off her two-piece, which isn't remotely useful in hiding her curves anyway. I'd rather tear those off her, but maybe I should try not to scare her.

She strokes my cock with her small hands. I free my own while her eyes widen and she stares at mine. Her gaze burns and makes it even harder to resist her.

I move closer to her and take her hand, putting it on my cock. She has a small hand that can't completely wrap around me. Her smooth skin warms me.

She runs her hand along my length. "Wow, I've never seen a cock like this."

I shiver. What does that mean? I don't have other beings commenting on my cock a lot. "Huh?"

She runs her fingers along the ridges on the top part of my cock and another hand strokes the bottom of my cock. "Look at these scaly parts down here."

Now... I don't know where this is leading up to. "Scaly?"

"Mmm hmm, these folds remind me of the underbelly of a dragon."

Her eyes are still glued to my cock with a faint smile. Her hands are shaking a little. Does this mean she doesn't like my cock? That'll be a bummer. I thought I had a pretty decent one...

She peeks at me. "I hope you know how to use this."

I groan. "I know how to use it amazingly well."

"Good."

She smiles with her legs spread, so I suppose this means she is looking forward to me. My cock twitches. I'm going to show her that she's my mate, and she is meant to be mine.

I rub her pussy. Her beautiful pink folds lure me. I rub my tip against her when she moans. She is soaking wet, probably ready for me. I've known a few humans, but I've never fucked one.

There are tinkles in my body and shouts for me to feel her folds. I press my tip into her and she squirms to spread her legs wider.

She groans. "Don't kill me with that cock."

"I won't. You'll die wanting more of me."

I push into her tight hole. Her walls squeeze me all at once. "So tight. Fuck..."

"Mmmm..." Her legs hike up to my side.

I should try my best not to hurt her. Her small body looks fragile, but the urge to grab her waist and pound into her is growing stronger and stronger.

She moans as I slide even more of my cock into her. When I reach something soft that stops me, she lets out a breath. Part of my cock is still outside, so... I pull a bit back and push forward. She screams and her body shudders.

"Um... Does it hurt?" That's the last thing I want.

She shakes my head. "Fuck, you have a long one."

So... That means I'm into the deepest part of her now. "Are you ready?"

She tries to smack me, but she can't reach my chest. So cute. I lean closer just to let her punch me.

"Fuck you! Get going already! You are already inside me and you're somehow still asking?"

I groan. She wants me. She wants my cock. I grab her waist and thrust into her. She moans every time I hit her deepest spot. It doesn't take long before I find where I should keep hammering.

"Fuck! Vikul! Dammit!" Her head is thrown back with her eyes shut as I rub that spot inside her. Her fingers dig into my back and it feels so right.

"You're sensitive here, huh?"

"Yes! Keep at it!" She squirms and her pussy squeezes me even harder. I slow my strokes, lengthening them to feel her folds. Her pussy is sucking me while her body shakes. There's nothing better than watching her arch to get more of me.

I slam into her again and again. She moans loudly with her body clinging around me.

"Fuck! I'm coming. Ahhh!" Her face twists and she holds me even tighter. "Fuck, you are so damn big. You're driving me crazy!"

Gosh... Her tight pussy squeezes me again. So perfect for me. "Come on my cock, come harder."

"Yes! Vikul!" She arches and thrusts herself at me.

I grunt. My cock is getting harder and I doubt I can hold it back for long. "I'm going to come inside you, fill you, and make you mine."

"Yes!"

Ha, this is easier than I thought. I know she is going to enjoy this and enjoy me.

I thrust into her a few more times, pounding my cock into the deepest part of her. She is so amazing, and I will never get tired of her.

I press in and pin myself to her while I empty my load into her. She moans and squirms. Her nails dig into me so hard that it almost hurts. Everything feels so right.

It's hard to imagine I ended up running into my mate on a foreign planet like this, but whatever fuels my spaceship.

My cock burns so hot inside her, pulsing in a way it has never done before. Maybe that's how I know she's my mate.

She gasps and stares at me with wide eyes. "Fuck, where did you get that vibrating cock?"

Vibrating? That's not what I'll describe about my cock, but she seems to like that. "Maybe I love you a bit too much."

"Hmm, flattering."

"Indeed."

The surge of heat keeps going inside of me. Her pussy squeezes me, taking every drop for herself. Her warmth wraps around me, making it almost impossible for me to pull out of her.

"Vikul... You're so hot."

I kiss her and she parts her lips. Our tongues tangle and further fan the fire in me.

My mate, finally.

Chapter 5

Galene

I open my eyes to a dark room and find myself on the bed. I don't remember falling asleep, but maybe I did after...

Vikul is sleeping by my side with his arm draping over me. He has a smile on his handsome sleeping face.

I let out a soft breath. He isn't as scary as I imagined and he isn't like the movies where aliens will kidnap humans and do scary experiments on them. Well... I hope that's not his plan.

My heart races when I stare at his muscular arm for another moment. I put the blanket back on me. The warmth inside me lingers. Maybe his cum is still warm in me, or it is the memory of how he fucked me.

I close my eyes, but I can see his cock in my mind. The ridges under his cock rubbed like hell. The good kind of hell. His cock has a nice curve upward and it stabbed at my sensitive spot every time he hammered into me.

I lift the blanket to peek at him. His cock is there, still wet with my juice. My cheek burns as I look at it. I can entertain the idea that aliens exist somewhere outside of Earth. The universe is probably a bit too big for humans to be the only special kind of beings.

But I never imagined I'd run into an alien and have his alien cock pounding my pussy.

His purple cock is there, looking real. My pleasure and his touches are very real too.

I blink and pull my eyes away from his cock, despite how hard it is. If he sees me peeking at his cock, he's going to be full of himself, as if he isn't already.

He didn't even talk to me before he grabbed me off the beach into his spaceship. There is no reason I should enjoy him as much as I did.

I take a deep breath, watching his face again. He seems completely oblivious to my stare. Ha, having such a good sleep after he kidnaped me and had his way with me.

I run my fingers along my chin. Something about this isn't right. He doesn't get to do whatever he wants. But...

His arm is still on my waist. I hold his wrist, but even that is too thick for my hand to wrap around completely. I lift his hand and try to get him off me, but his arm is heavy.

My cheek burns when I can't shake the memory of him towering over my tiny body with his huge, muscular ass, pounding away at me.

He must have used something on me and made me horny. Otherwise, there's no way I'd fall for his silly move. He has a cock. That's all about it.

"What are you doing?" His eyes open and I flinch.

I'm still holding his arm and I'm halfway in moving him off me, but...

He flashes his teeth at me, but it isn't a smile. "Are you trying to flee? Even though I've told you that we're on my spaceship and there's no place you can go?"

"Oh... No... I... I want to run to the washroom."

"Ah... Sure."

He sits up and stretches his arms. Maybe that's from the soreness of laying in bed, or maybe he wants to flex his muscles at me.

He has perfectly chiseled back muscles and when he flexes, he makes for a pretty great view.

I silently kick myself. This isn't the time to admire his figure. He kidnapped me! I should remember that instead of what he can do to me.

He gets off the bed and gestures for me to go with him. "I'll show you where the washroom is."

I suppose that's fair. It isn't like he's going to let me wander around and accidentally go somewhere I shouldn't.

There should be buttons to open the door and get outside of the spaceship. I won't attempt to expose my-self to the vacuum of space and who knows whatever radiation outside that may kill me within seconds, but if I'm left on my own...

Maybe I shouldn't wander around on my own. I wouldn't even trust myself to figure out the spaceship.

I get off the bed when he is standing there with his eyes closed and his arms folded. Maybe he is still sleepy and is trying to steal a brief moment for himself.

Isn't he cute with that? I suppose he can tell me where the washroom is, then he won't have to get out of bed.

He is standing there with his cock dangling between his legs. That huge monster seems to be the same size as when he was having a go with me, except it isn't erected into that juicy angle.

No! I'm not supposed to be staring at his cock. Maybe that's why he is standing with his eyes closed. He thinks that I'm going to stare at his cock and think that he is amazing or something.

He shudders and shakes his head. "Ah, sorry. Let's get going."

Now, he is pretending to know nothing about his little prank. Maybe he thinks I'd know nothing about that, except I see through that. He is a showy alien who thinks his cock is amazing, so amazing that he gets to do whatever he wants.

He has no intention of putting on trousers. Maybe he is going to walk around completely naked. I refuse to look at him. He isn't looking at me, but making his way to the door.

If I refuse to look at him and he finds out about that, will he think that it's because I'm too shy? Or maybe he will think that he caught me staring and I should turn my gaze elsewhere?

Maybe I should just walk like a normal person.

He arrives at the door and puts his hand on the wall to the side, searching for the obvious button. It takes him a few seconds before he finds it. I understand different species have different sensations about things, but he should be able to see in this room. Maybe he's half-asleep again.

The door slides open, and we are back in the corridor again. He takes a few steps down the corridor, shakily.

On the walls, there are a few spots with display windows, as if I'm walking inside a museum. Inside the display boxes, there are pieces of minerals. The corridor is dim, but there is light inside those boxes.

I walk past one with a piece of rock the size of my fist. It is a black rock that looks like obsidian, but infused with some silver patches that aren't the reflection of light. Maybe this rock is worth a lot and is part of his collection.

The next rock is red, looks like just a ruby. There is white light shining on it and...

I rub my eyes and take a step closer to the display window. There seems to be a weak glow of red from the stone. It looks like mist, but... That's interesting.

Oof!

I bump into him. He shouldn't have stopped without a warning.

He points at the opened door. "There you go. Watch your steps, otherwise..." He smirks and seems to be a bit more energetic now, which I'm not sure whether that's a good thing for me.

"Thank you." I go inside before he will decide to get in with me.

The light of the washroom turns on when I enter. It is a nice and clean place with a shower area and a toilet on the other side. The floor is made of marble-like material. The mineral component seems different, but it has a glint like marble and is white.

I wasn't planning to go to the washroom, but while I'm here...

The wall of the washroom is like the floor. This place looks expensive and I feel out of place.

Wait...

Is Vikul waiting outside?

I'm not sure whether I want to go back to the room with him. But even though the washroom is pretty clean, I don't feel like staying here either.

I stand on my tip toe to barely reach the tap for water. I wash my hands in front of the window above the sink.

In the mirror, my eyes are barely open, and my shoulders are slumping.

There are faint marks from the sun on me, but not a lot when I probably didn't get to lie on the beach for long before Vikul kidnapped me. Maybe the sudden surge of tiredness was because of him.

He can't be the only alien that can reach Earth, and if he can do that, he probably has advanced technology. Having something that can make me drowsy and fall asleep isn't out of the realm of possibility.

I wonder what that technology is intended for. It can't be for him to kidnap other beings, right?

Can't say I'm flattered by that even though he insisted on how he wanted me to be here.

Where is this spaceship going? Back to his planet? On the way to another planet?

I hold on to the sink and support my weight with my arms as I try to get a better view of myself from the mirror. This place is designed for someone like him, not me.

I still... look a bit too thick and don't have the perfect beach body ready.

Among all the women on the beach, I can't be the most attractive one. Why did Vikul kidnap me and not someone else?

I let out a soft sigh. It's not like I'd wish for someone else to be kidnapped, but—

Someone, Vikul, knocks on the door. "Are you done? Did you fall asleep? Get out of there!" He's almost growling by the end of the sentence, so I better hurry.

"I'm washing my hands."

He murmurs something, but his voice is too soft for me to pick up the words.

I go to the door and tap the button for it to open. The moment it opens, he dashes through the door. He almost bumps into me. I jump to the side right before he will run into me. With his huge body, he will smash me like a truck.

I'm about to shout at him until... Well, I suppose I'm not the only one needing the washroom.

Fuck... Why am I standing here watching him?

I turn around and get out of the door. "I'm heading back to the room now."

"No, you wait for me outside." He remains standing there, managing his business, which is probably the only reason he isn't chasing me already.

"Fine..." The door has already closed behind me, so I raise my voice.

Other than having sex with an alien, I'm also waiting outside of the washroom for an alien. Can life get even crazier?

When he finally comes out of the washroom, I'm getting bored. He squints at me while I turn around and head back to the room.

He grunts. "It looks like you don't want to talk to me now."

"Yes, you kidnapped me."

"You didn't seem to remember them when I had you pinned under me."

I suck in a breath, trying my best to keep walking down the corridor. My cheek burns hot and the surge of heat inside me is coming back. I should have known he was going to mention that again.

"I'm tired."

"Well, fine."

Chapter 6

Vikul

I have no idea what's wrong with Galene. It seems like she is mad at me. She said that she was tired, but I don't believe that at all. She just wanted some time to herself, which... I will learn to let her.

After so much happening and how I got her here with me, maybe she gets to be a bit mad at me.

I check the time again and check the map. We are getting closer to where the portal is probably going to show up. According to the forecast, there is a ninety-percent chance for that to happen on time.

When we got back into my bedroom, Galene went straight to the bed and grabbed the blanket for herself. I joined her on the bed, but she refused to look at me. She also refused to give me part of the blanket. Given that it's my blanket, she is rude.

Maybe that's the way humans exert their dominance.

By... taking the whole blanket and occupying the center of the bed?

I let out a soft sigh. I don't understand humans, after all. While she tried to occupy the whole bed, she had forgotten how it was designed for a being my size, not hers, so despite her spreading her arms and legs, I still managed enough room for myself.

Women... Interesting.

I shrug and sit back in my chair, leaning onto the back-rest. She is my mate now. Maybe everything happened a bit too quickly for her so she'll need some more time.

For me, I found her. But for her, she has to learn about aliens at the same time.

I lift my hand, staring at my purple skin. I don't think I look that strange. She's the one making it dramatic.

I close my eyes and all I can see is her naked body. She has the perfect curves and the perfect smile. Everything about her is just right. I've never been with a being her size. She makes it easy to hold in my arms and to pin down on the bed.

My cock twitches. Maybe I want her again. Weird how she has that kind of effect on me.

I tap on the screen and look at my work schedule. I have to be back home soon to deposit the order, which is safe in the storage room now.

Will she get used to life outside of Earth? There will be a lot of other species around, which is probably the main difference.

But she has to stay with me. She is my mate and I refuse to be separated from her. I run my fingers along the dashboard. Among all the planets out there, there has to be one she will enjoy staying on. Moving to a different planet would be annoying, but if that's what she wants, I'm going to do that. Everything for my mate.

Chapter 7

Galene

Despite lying in the comfortable bed, I can't fall asleep. Vikul isn't around and I should treasure the time to myself.

This bed is mine, and the room is mine, at least until he is back.

It is another day now. I still have no idea what is happening and where this spaceship is heading.

All I know is Vikul wants to make me his mate, and he doesn't care what I think.

So annoying. I'm not an item for him to decide what to use me for.

Staying here in the room is boring. Maybe Vikul thinks that he can punish me by leaving me alone with nothing better to do other than staring at the walls and looking out of the window at the darkness out there. There are stars outside and it is a beautiful scene. But however beautiful it is, it gets boring soon.

The map on the wall across from the bed is still a mystery. Maybe it's the map of Vikul's home planet or home city, that will make more sense.

There is a desk to the side, but there isn't a thing on it, and also nothing in the drawers.

Boring...

I lie on the bed again, spreading my arms and legs to the side. I don't like this place. Space traveling is so boring. Does Vikul do this a lot? If so, he may have patience that I don't have.

Stupid Vikul and his purple ass... Instead of staring at the ceiling and resting on a bed like I do every single day back in my own place, I could be sunbathing and enjoying the beach.

I close my eyes to recall the warmth of the sun and the gentle breeze on the beach. A lump forms in my chest when I mourn the loss of my vacation. Not only is the vacation gone, but my life on Earth is also pretty much gone.

Vikul is a crazy purple being who kidnaps other beings, and he isn't going to put me back on Earth...

There are so many things I haven't done on Earth...

There is a faint hiss at the door. I open my eyes to Vikul and his stupid purple body is there by the bed again. I huff and look away from him.

"Galene..."

I ignore him and refuse to give him a reaction.

The bed shudders when he sits his ass on it despite how I'm trying my best to take up space. This is his spaceship and maybe it makes no sense for me to attempt to get the whole bed for myself, but I can't stop myself. I have no interest in sleeping next to him.

Though… He has still been sleeping here because the bed is a bit too big for me to completely occupy.

He climbs over and straddles me.

I groan. "What are you doing?"

"Missing your soft body."

Fuck…

As if triggered by his words, there is a small spark inside my chest, spreading to my pussy and burning even harder than before. It feels like the first time I met him. There is a pull that draws me to him.

When he straddles me, he seems to be even larger. The bulge in his trousers… Dammit…

I can't pull my eyes away from him when he smirks at me. He must have caught me staring at him…

"Liking what you see and will get?"

I huff and roll to face the other side. "Go away, I don't want you."

"Are you sure?" He leans closer with his warm breath on my face.

I take a deep breath when the fire in me burns even hotter. His body is so close to me that it will be tempting to give in to my desire.

Vikul is so fucking annoying, but my body wants him… That's so wrong.

I close my eyes, but all I can see is how he made me come.

"Galene," he says in a voice that vibrates within me, lighting all my sensations. "Who are you denying?"

I roll onto my stomach, getting myself as far away from him as I can when I can't get out of bed. He has me locked between his legs. He is kneeling on the bed, straddling me, and... the heat from his body is driving me crazy.

He packs a kiss on my earlobe, and I shudder. "I won't force you and I won't make you do things you hate. But trust me, you want me. Your body is a lot more honest than your mind."

Fuck him... I clench a fist, trying to scream at my body. I don't need him and...

Dammit... He annoys me. I suppose he hasn't touched me yet, but... I rub my pussy against the bed when lust burns even stronger in me. It feels like his cock is hovering right behind me, mere inches from my ass.

"Galene, you make me hard, so hard it hurts."

I roll around. "Fine, you have to be annoying, huh?"

He smirks and his cock twitches. The monster is still in his trousers, but it is threatening to fuck me hard and make me come like a little slut for him.

"I know what you want. You just don't want to admit it to yourself. Don't you feel it inside you?"

My heart pounds inside my chest and can jump out of my throat at any second. He isn't wrong. There is a pull in me that screams for how I can enjoy the pleasure he gives me.

I'm on his spaceship anyway. Space travel is boring and... He is going to give me more pleasure than I can imagine.

As if reading my mind, he leans closer and cups my cheek in his hands. His chest almost pressed into my boobs. "I want you. Just the thought of you has been burning me from the inside for the whole day."

I suck in a breath, only for his scent to smack me in the head. I rub his cock with my knees when I can't reach him with my hand. "You are so hard, so huge."

He lets out a soft moan. "Hard for you. Please?"

He grabs my boobs and kisses me over the bikini top. His lips are so hot that he may as well set my bikini on fire. He knows what he is doing, and that's so annoying. I should try to resist him, not getting rid of his trousers with my toes. Dammit.

"Galene, you are so perfect." He takes off my bikini top and sucks on my nipple, pinching the other as if he hasn't teased me enough.

His cock weighs on my pussy and when he moves to lick my boobs, he is rubbing against my clit with his heat, but doing nothing to quench the lust in me.

There is an urge in me that screams for me to arch and move. His cock is almost right in front of my entrance. But... So much for resisting him. He already thinks he has the perfect cock that I somehow can't wait to get more.

I'm not going to stroke his ego, definitely not!

He flips me over and puts me on my stomach. "I've been wanting this for so long."

"You are no help, horny beyond repair. Oof—!" A moan escapes me when he rubs my pussy with his rough hand. He has a large hand and when he flicks my clit... He could make me come with his fingers alone.

"You are soaking wet, so much so you are dripping your sweet juice. As if I'm the only one wanting this?"

"Shut up and fuck me already." My cheek is burning hot and I hate to say that. But...

"I know you are a horny little slut for my cock."

He grabs my waist and pushes his thick tip into me. His tip stretches me, but his ridges rub into me, slamming in the pleasure before he even starts fucking with me. The scales under his cock follow and—

Fuck... When he thrusts in from behind, he feels even larger.

"You are so tight. Your pussy squeezing me..." He gasps and his hot breath warms me. He grabs my boobs, wrapping his arms around me, enveloping my whole body with his.

He rides me from behind, pounding his cock deep into me. With the fucking annoying curvature of his cock, his ridges rub right onto my sensitive spot again and again. He must have found it and remembered it from the last time. I'm a mushy pile after a few thrusts. I can't even resist him with my mind.

"Vikul..."

His cock is pulsing and twitching. And his ridges...

He slams into me, again and again and again, until I'm losing my mind. All I know is how his cock devours me and makes me his slut. I hate it, but I can't stop the orgasm rushing through me.

Not that I really hate it, but... How can he make me come this easily? It makes no sense.

I scream and squirm. My legs are shaking and I don't know what to do with my hands.

My brain is fried and all I can think about is how good he is fucking me. He slams his huge cock into my pussy and pulls it out, ramming it into me again. With his huge body, he dominates me. All I can do is let him hold me down and do whatever he wants to me.

"Look at you, coming on my cock. Time for you to accept how you can't live without me."

He thrusts into me again and again, making me come whenever he wants. I can't even take a breath.

But the pleasure is so good that I don't want him to stop. "Fuck you!"

"I know you love being my little slut."

I punch the bed when I can't reach him. The pleasure is so strong that I can't even control my body. Fuck... How can he make me such a mess?

"Fuck you..."

I move and try to roll around, not expecting success when his cock is buried deep into me, but he lets me. He rolls over and pulls me on top of him.

I'm going to be his slut, but it's going to be my way. He doesn't get to do whatever he wants and he can't be the one making a messy pile.

He smiles as if he thinks I'm only as good as his fuck-toy. But I'm going to be the one calling the shots. He can't be the only one that can mess with me. He can keep imagining himself with a magical cock that I'm going to crave.

I grab his shoulders and lift myself, then slam my pussy down on his cock. His thick cock rubs me so hard that I almost come at the moment. My pussy squeezes him and he groans.

His cock twitches inside me as if showing off his thickness. "It looks like you have something good for me."

I ride him harder and faster, taking more of him in every time. He is getting harder and when he is such a huge alien; he makes me look tiny while I ride his cock.

And his fucking cock... Those scales and his ridges are killing me.

He laughs. "Looks like before you can make me come, you are going to come first; like a perfect little slut who has no self-control."

I punch his chest, but he doesn't seem to even feel it. I grit my teeth, fighting to hold back my pleasure. I slam my hips up and down, grinding his cock. His tip thrust right into the deepest of me.

He grabs me and rolls us around. Before I can get away, he pins me down and thrust into me.

He holds me down, and pounds me harder and faster, making me scream.

"Fuck you, Vikul, you've been waiting."

"I've let you try, but you see, this is what's called pleasure, my cute little human."

I shake my head and bite my lower lip. But when he fucks me with his huge cock, it is getting harder by the second. The way he rubs into me is so good, and those ridges are fucking driving me crazy. I'm not going to let him think he is better than me, but...

If he keeps going, will I die from pleasure?

With his huge body, he doesn't seem to need a break, but...

"Vikul!"

"Admit it!" He grunts and his cock twitches again.

Fuck... I can't stop the pleasure from coming for me. I scream as an orgasm hits me. I've only met this single alien, but he is certainly the most arrogant and frustrating alien that ever existed.

He nibbles on my throat. "No one has ever made you come like this."

The problem is, I know I can stop him, but I don't want to stop him when the pleasure is draining my sanity.

"Vikul! Fuck!" I scream again when he thrusts in another wave of pleasure. I wrap my legs around him. "Come in me."

"Really? I can't hear you." He chuckles. Maybe this is his plan all along, fucking me so hard that I'd beg for his cum.

I don't think I need to, but my body craves him — just the way he wants. How did this even happen...?

"Vikul, please! Give me your cum."

"As you wish, my mate." He grunts and thrusts into the deepest part of me, pulsing in his hot cum.

I grit my teeth, containing the pleasure before that will break me into pieces. This time, it takes him even longer before he empties his balls.

"You are a fucking crazy alien."

"And you love that."

I hate him so much...

He pulls out of me and puts my head on the pillow and my body on the bed. "Hmm... I love you so much."

Except all I want to do is smack him. He thinks that he is better than me with his huge body and that annoying cock...

He kisses my forehead again before he gets off the bed. "I'll bring you water. Have some rest."

He covers me with the blanket. Right at the door, he turns around to watch me for another second before he leaves.

I hold the blanket, swearing at his back under my breath. Fuck him... He keeps doing things to me, and worse, I hate how much I love that...

Chapter 8

Vikul

"Wake up!" I pull the blanket away from Galene. "How long have you been sleeping?"

She groans and opens her eyes. She is still naked and has been with the blanket since the last time we fucked and she rode my cock, which had been a while by now. "Longer than you want and I don't care about what you want."

She was enjoying herself the last time I fucked her. She wanted that and screamed how much she wanted me to come inside her. Yet, she started acting like this the other morning until now.

She refuses to talk to me and she almost kicked my balls last night when I tried to get into my bed. I wasn't even planning to fuck her. And the other day, she almost breathed fire, so fierce that I didn't even dare to tempt her.

What's wrong with her?

I sigh. "Well, are you going to tell me what's wrong or am I going to have to make a guess?"

She glares at me as if I should know what's wrong already. Is this how women function?

She balls herself and rolls to the side, refusing to look at me. "I've told you. You kidnapped me and I don't even know where we are going. You've never told me your plan or why you kidnapped me. All you care about is fucking me. I hate that."

I roll my eyes. I told her a while ago. Did she forget about it? Or is she looking for whatever excuses she can grab to be mad at me over nothing?

"I've told you already. We are heading to my home. Other than taking you here, I didn't have another way. By now, you should know you are my mate and that's why you are here. I have no other plans other than that."

She groans. "Geez, get your mind out of the gutter."

Except I don't understand. I wasn't thinking about fucking her at this moment and she hasn't been in a mood for me to feel good asking for that. I can't say that I don't want her, though. But I know better than asking when she is clearly pissed.

I clear my throat. "We are landing soon. You are going to enjoy staying with me."

She huffs. "I want to go back to Earth."

"Why?" It pains me. I thought she knows how much she wants me and how we can be together perfectly.

Can't she feel the bond between us? Why is she denying that?

I give her my hand. "Come with me? I will show you everything. The ship, my place, and everything I own."

"And I'm going to walk around naked."

Oh, hell no. Her naked body is for me alone, so no one else gets to see that. "Don't worry about that. I will have clothes for you in my place and we won't meet a single being before I get you clothed."

She looks at my hand but makes no move to take it. Do humans not do something like that?

"Galene..."

Her gaze flicks to the side again as if I'm not worth looking at. I grit my teeth, resisting the urge to yell at her. Yelling or growling at her won't help the situation. Maybe I made her come here, but she should understand it by now.

I hiss regardless; that's the least I can do. "I have to go back to the driving seat soon. Why don't you come with me? Otherwise, I'll have to move you alongside the blanket."

She remains quiet as if she didn't even hear me.

I click my tongue. "Are you cold?"

"Maybe."

What does that mean?

She isn't looking at me. I can only hope she will get out of her mood soon. Silly woman. While she is my mate, that makes her kind of cute, but I'd rather see her smile.

I go to the wardrobe, pressing the button for the door to open. I only have clothes for myself, but maybe there will be something that fits her.

I pick up a T-shirt. It is probably too large for her, but it will hide her curves. I toss it to her alongside a pair of shorts. Maybe those will be long enough to pass as trousers for her.

She picks up the clothes and finally starts dressing. My phone beeps and I pull it to check. It is the spaceship calling. I have to be there to oversee the landing.

I head to the door. "When you are ready, come join me at the dashboard. Get out of the room and turn left, go all the way down the corridor and you will find me behind the door."

I head to the door and get out of the room. In theory, the system can do the landing, but I'm required to oversee it in order to avoid errors and extra payments for repairing the spaceship. I'm going to sit at the dashboard and pay attention.

Someone should invent a better way, then I won't have to take my eyes off her.

Chapter 9

Galene

I put on the clothes he tossed me, swearing under my breath. The longer I stay, the more I hate this place. This spaceship probably cost a lot, but for me, this is just a jail.

I put on my bikini and move on to put on his T-shirt, which is too large for me. I suck in a breath to calm myself, but all I get is his scent. My cheek burns at that. I hate how I can't shake his naked body out of my mind.

Why must I care about him?

I fold my arms after I put on the trousers. It should be a pair of shorts for him, but a bit too long for me. While he said that we won't run into anyone else, I don't want to take the risk. I don't even want to be seen in a bikini.

Fuck...

He said that I'm his mate, but why would he want me? Maybe that's just like what I've thought, it is just a game for when we fuck around. He could have been with someone else. Someone his species, or someone who looks better than me.

I get off the bed. I'll have to join him at the dashboard if I don't want to have a huge purple alien shouting at my face again. He just wants to do whatever he wants to.

He mentioned landing. I'm probably far away from Earth by now. I have nothing with me. There's no way I can leave and stay alive. I just wish I could go back to Earth. But knowing Vikul, he isn't going to let that happen.

He wants to show me his stuff, thinking that he is amazing or something, except I don't even care.

Chapter 10

Vikul

"Hey..."

I turn around to see Galene standing by the door. I gesture for her to come over. She looks perfect in my clothes. Well, not that the clothes remotely fit her, but... Something about watching her in my clothes makes me hard. It feels like I'm holding her in my arms, even though I'm not.

She is looking out of the window. She doesn't know about other beings outside of Earth and probably has never been away from Earth, either.

I point at the window. We are in the city already, finally, in familiar terrain for me. "We will arrive soon."

She gets closer and closer to the window until the dashboard stops her from sticking her nose in the window. "So... That's an alien city."

"You can say that. If you have gotten out of the room earlier, you could have looked at the planet, but there will be time."

She falls silent. It seems like she doesn't like it when I mention her stay with me. That's probably because she doesn't know anything about me, yet. When she knows what I can provide her with, she will understand and will want to stay with me.

She is still looking outside of the window. Maybe she finds the pointy buildings interesting. These buildings bore me and most of the time, I don't even look at them when I've seen these so many times.

The busiest place in the city is right beyond us. There are other spaceships flying. I press the button and turn the spaceship to merge with one of the paths that will lead us home.

"So... Even in the city, you drive spaceships," she says.

"It doesn't matter as long as you don't take up space and block the path. I sometimes swap to another ship if I have no intention of flying to another planet. Smaller ships use less fuel."

"Are spaceships expensive?"

I chuckle. "Not very expensive. It depends on what you want. I can teach you how to drive one and you can pick whatever you like."

"Whatever I like? Are you sure about that?" She turns around with a surprised look.

I shrug. "Yes, whatever you want. Price isn't an issue for my mate."

She stares at me, long and hard until I can't sit still in my seat. I lift an eyebrow at her. "What's the issue? Do you not believe me?"

She holds up a hand. "Wait... You really think that I'm your mate."

"Yes, I know you are. You may not understand that at this moment, but it is fine. We have time and maybe you will understand that soon enough, or eventually, either is fine with me."

She stares at me, scared and worried. I frown, but I fight to keep my face neutral. I ask, "What are you worried about? Living in a new place? Scared of me?"

She says nothing and goes back to window-staring.

I let out a soft sigh, hoping she won't hear it. She is so confusing.

As we get closer to my place, I slow the ship and get us ready for landing. I pat my lap. "Sit; it may be shaky when we land."

"I can stand on my own."

"I don't understand. I know I kidnapped you and you aren't happy about that. But that's in the past now. Why don't you enjoy our time together instead? You know you've enjoyed me. Who are we fooling?"

She shakes her head without moving a step. "I said I'm going to be fine standing here."

I've already shoved my cock into her and made her come more than once, but somehow, she doesn't even want to sit on my lap. It isn't like there are other beings around. What's she worried about?

"Fine. If you fall, I'm not going to pick you up." I pull the lever and step on the peddle, getting ready as we get to the parking site for the apartment building.

My spaceship floats in the air, waiting for the door on the ground to open before I descend. The spaceship shudders a tiny bit when the wheels touch the floor.

The light for the tunnel leading to the parking lot lights up as I drive us through it. She is still looking outside. "Looks like a parking lot on Earth, but you park spaceships instead of cars."

"Yeah." Now, I'm the one who doesn't want to talk to her. She thinks that she gets to be rude and gets to do whatever she wants because she is my mate. How disrespectful.

We get out of the spaceship and take the lift to my apartment. When we are finally at my door, she is still a few steps behind me, busy looking at my collection along the corridor. This floor is mine alone, so there won't be any other beings interrupting me.

I reach my palm to the keypad when she asks, "You have a lot of rocks here."

"Yes. Do you like them?" I show my palm and the door opens. I get inside while she is still staring at my prized piece of ivriel. "It is ivriel."

"Oh... What's the use of it? The deep blue looks pretty good."

"Well, it is hard, and a slightly cheaper alternative to diamonds when it comes to industrial usage. It doesn't have a shine like the other stones that are commonly used for jewelry, though." I go over to the display and point at it. "Look at this part, where there is the black."

"Mmmhmm?"

"That's where the magma of the planet infused into this ivriel. A rare occurrence. And if you look closely to the side, you can check out the special structure here. Most ivriel is striated, but this one is the other way around."

She blinks and she shudders, taking a step back while holding her nose. "Ouch..."

I resist the urge to laugh. She is so cute.

She rubs her nose and rolls her eyes. "You better not be messing with me about the stone."

"I'm not. You can check out more inside my place."

My heart swells when she finally stops frowning at me. She has a faint smile and a spark in her eyes, maybe she is interested in minerals. That will be a great start. I still have stock to unload, but that can wait. Now, all I want to do is to stay with her and make her happy.

Chapter 11

Galene

Vikul brings me along, and we walk through rooms upon rooms with stones and rocks. It seems like this whole floor is his. He keeps introducing me to the gemstones and statues made from rare stones. They're impressive and make it seem like I'm in a museum instead of an apartment.

He keeps talking and talking while I'm no longer paying attention to him. He is excited about everything he owns and he wants to share those with me. But I don't really care about that.

All he cares about is what he wants. He doesn't seem to care about me. I don't understand the mate thing, but I doubt it means any good for me. Maybe all he wants is to keep me here in his home, just like how he keeps his collection here.

This is a large apartment. The tiles on the floor are black with silver sparkles, just like the ones on the ceiling. The walls are a very faint gray, almost white, making this place brighter despite the dim light. The lights in the display boxes are brighter. He is such a show-off.

There are couches and a dining table, but this place has so few items that it feels like he doesn't even live here. Or maybe he is a bit too tidy with his stuff.

I halt right before I bump into him. He stops in the path for no reason again...

He is frowning at me. "Do you have any questions?"

I shake my head. "No, all is good."

"Your face doesn't say that. What's up?"

"Nothing. I'm just looking around."

He cups my face in his hands and nudges me to look at him. "I thought you liked the minerals and stones."

"You like your collection."

He grins, proudly. "Yes, I do."

"I know." I turn away from him. "I'm tired."

"Why are you always tired? You just woke up before we landed."

I shrug. "No idea why."

"Well..." He sighs. "I suppose you can go and take a rest in your room. Maybe I should get you better-fitting clothes, too."

"I don't want anything from you. I just want to go back to Earth." I sigh after I said the words. It doesn't seem like he will care anyway.

"Why? Do you not like this place?"

I shake my head. "You won't understand. I know you are rich and everything, but... Never mind, I just want to be on my own if you aren't letting me go back to Earth."

He grunts and wraps his arms around me, pulling me to his chest. I want to push him away, but it won't be useful. Maybe he'd think I'm playing with him. I let him hug me, but I won't move an inch and I won't hug him back.

He is a huge male and his body lights a flame inside me. There is a pulse of heat between my legs. But...

"Galene, talk to me. Something is wrong. Are you sick?"

I let out a breath when he finally let go of me. Maybe he figured I'm not in the mood to hug him or do anything with him. "Maybe homesick."

He stares at me. "Do you... really want to go back to Earth? Because I took you here without asking you about that first?"

I nod. "I can't be your mate. I'm a human, and you aren't."

He grunts. "That doesn't matter. I know you are my mate and I can feel it inside my blood."

There is a spark inside me, which echoes his words. Maybe he is my mate, but I don't want to be his.

I shake my head again. "I'm..." I spread my arms to the side. Being in his size of clothing still makes me feel huge and weird. "I bet there are better females to be your mate."

He growls. "What do you mean? You are perfect!"

I shiver and snap my head up at him.

He takes a step back. "Sorry, I don't mean to scare you, but I don't understand what you mean. Why will there be better females to be my mate?"

"Well, there are some that are..." I stare at my stomach. When I'm standing, it isn't as apparent, but... "Someone that looks better than me. You are a handsome trocul, so you should find someone, well, better looking than me."

He sucks in a breath, as if he is trying to take part of my soul with him. He slowly lets his breath out while I brace myself for him to scream at me.

He clears his throat. "I still don't understand. Which part of you isn't good-looking enough?"

My cheek burns. No one has said something like that to me before. "I mean, it's like..."

"Ah, you think you are fat or something."

"Yeah..." I grimace when it hurts. That's what I mean to say, but I can't make myself say it out loud. "So... I won't look good on you and—"

"Who said you are fat?"

Well... A lot of people? Maybe we were just kids and kids made fun of each other and I should get over it, but... I've always been on the chubbier side.

He leans over, getting closer to me. "I'm asking. Who said that to you?"

"What are you asking that for?"

He clenches a fist. "I'm going to make them regret it."

"Oh..."

"No one gets to say that to you. You have the perfect curves for me, and I don't care what others said about you. If they dare to say that, I'm going to show them red. Well, or blue, or whatever color their blood is."

He has a deep scowl on his face, and he doesn't seem to be joking at all.

He continues, "I won't let anyone insult my mate. Ah... It seems like you haven't agreed to that, so I'm taking that back. But still, no one gets to call you that."

I... While I appreciate that, I'm still not sure what to think about being his mate.

He sighs. "I thought we had that figured out already."

Maybe when he asked me as we were having sex, he meant it, but I didn't see it that way.

He holds my hand. "Tell me what you think? Please? Do you not like how I'm purple?"

I burst out laughing, even though I probably shouldn't. "This is crazy."

"So purple is fine, right? You make me conscious of how I look. I love your curves and it looks like you will enjoy food with me. But there's no way I can change my color."

Maybe I was being silly with how I'm not the thinnest woman ever. I move my hand to my stomach and pinch myself when he groans again.

I shrug. "Fine, no mention of my size again, right?"

"Yes, unless you want me to grab your small body and pound your pussy, then I don't mind."

Fuck him... My body burns again and I can't stop the memory of his huge cock fucking me seeps into my mind.

"You can never get your mind out of the gutter."

He hugs me so tightly to him that he can almost choke me. "Please, give me a chance. I will show you how I really want you as my mate and I intend to take good care of you."

I can feel the heat inside his body as if it is mine. The something that seems to link us together is there again, but...

He rubs my back. "What do you want? If you don't like this place, we can move somewhere else. We can check out the cities on this planet. If you don't find anything you love, we will go and look at other planets until you are somewhere you enjoy."

That... I don't know how much things cost here, but I suppose owning an entire floor of an apartment building isn't going to be cheap even though we aren't on Earth. "Sounds like you are rich."

"There are always being richer out there. I live a life I enjoy, which I built with my own hands, and I want to share everything I have with you."

He kneels on a knee, putting me taller than him. "Please? I know I never asked you before I took you from the beach on Earth. Or..." He sighs. "Do you really want to go back to Earth?"

"What if that's what I want?"

His shoulders slump. "I suppose I can't stop you from wanting that. I don't want you to be sad and stay here just because I want you to."

"Ha, didn't figure that. You've been doing whatever you want."

My heart skips a beat when he lifts his brows at me with tension inside his body. I probably should remember how he is a lot larger than me and he can punch me or beat me easily.

"I can understand that humans and I experience things differently. I'll miss you a lot. I can't be on Earth, so... In theory, I shouldn't have been to Earth. I wouldn't have found you. You are my mate, the only one in the whole universe. I'd like to think I'm a pretty good male, but..."

"You mean you won't make me stay?"

"I figured there's no point in doing that." He turns to the living room, gesturing everything around the apartment. "Faintly, I knew that my mate was somewhere out there. Every trocul has a mate, but not everyone ends up with their mate. I've never given that a lot of thought until I saw you, and until I felt the connection between us. Please? Give me a chance?"

Now that he says it like that... He isn't the first male I've ever dated. I've never felt something like that either.

Should I... Give him a try? Give "us" a chance?

Chapter 12

Vikul

My apartment seems to grow colder by the second and is getting freezing cold in no time. My blood can freeze at any moment as I watch Galene ponder.

I've been through negotiations with trade partners, competitions, and governments, but none of those are as scary as this.

I take a deep breath while trying my best to look calm. That has been what I do when I have to negotiate. Better not let the other party know that I'm dying for the deal and I really want it.

But Galene isn't my trading partner. She will be my mate as soon as she agrees.

I'm a lot larger than her, but the way she looks at me... It feels like I have to hide somewhere and I'm not good enough.

She is still quiet and I have to bite my tongue to keep quiet. I have already asked, it is time to wait for her answer.

"Um... Vikul..."

"Yes?" My heart races and I brace myself for her answer. She doesn't seem to be certain, and she doesn't seem relieved. Does that mean she would rather go back to Earth? She understands that I won't be able to stay with her if that's the case, right?

She hasn't given me the answer, yet... It feels like she is holding my heart in her small hands, weighing it, and deciding whether I'm good enough for her.

Fuck... This is so hard.

"What will happen if I agree to be your mate? What will I be doing? I hope you aren't planning to fuck me all the time."

I roll my eyes, though my cock twitches, clearly liking that idea. "I wish, but I have a job. So no, I won't be fucking you all the time. Disappointed?"

She takes a deep breath as if considering it. "What's your job? Kidnapping?"

I groan. How dare she think of me as someone like that? I've only kidnapped a single being, and that's her. I couldn't stop myself and I couldn't afford to miss out on her. "No. If that's my job, I'd be a lot richer."

She laughs. "I'm imagining you running around, kidnapping beings, and trying to impress them with your cock."

My cheek burns and a tingle travels down my spine. Does she know what she is talking about? Fuck... She is such a tease. The urge to pin her on some surface and fuck her until she screams is so strong.

"I know you are impressed with my cock, but that's not the point. I'm a trader of minerals and I travel planets to look for things I can sell."

Her eyes widen at me as if she has never expected that to be a job. Do humans not trade? Do they not set up shops and factories?

She says, "Sounds like you travel a lot."

"I used to travel more, but recently, a bit less when my business is going pretty well. Complacency has no place in business, though. I still go places and that's why I ran into you. Earth is a pretty exotic place, though most of the things I've seen aren't interesting enough. Not worth breaking the rules for."

"Breaking what rules?"

"Ah, did I not tell you I'm not supposed to be on Earth at all?"

"Because everyone will stare at you and laugh at your purple ass for being in a Halloween mood before the day is remotely close."

I don't know what Halloween is. Maybe it's a human festival. There aren't a lot of humans living on this planet, so that's off my radar. "That. And also, humans on Earth aren't supposed to know of our existence. Us as in beings outside of Earth."

She folds her arms and rolls her eyes at that. "Said the one who went to Earth regardless and took me here."

"Yeah, it is an unspoken rule, but we wait for planets to have the technology to find us, not the other way. I think that's for us to see what each planet will come up with on its own instead of influencing them with what we have. Otherwise, that's going to make everything the same and boring. I was on the way to deliver things, but waiting in the space with nothing to do got boring."

I have no idea whether she understands that or not, but there's hope she does.

She shrugs. "Still doesn't tell me what is going to happen if I become your mate."

I grit my teeth to stop myself from saying that she already is my mate, whether she likes it or not. But I suppose she can refuse to admit it and leave with a piece of my soul with her. "You will stay with me and we will travel together. You can have everything I have and everything you want."

She watches me with cautious eyes again.

I spread my hands to the side. "I mean it. I will give you everything."

"Sounds like there is a catch there."

Ah... A bit too good to be true to her? "We probably won't be on Earth a lot, if ever. If that counts as a catch? There are a lot more planets we can go to, though. Tell me where you want to go and we can be there in no time."

She has a wicked smirk on her face... My heart races and the blood drains from my head. Apparently, I said the wrong thing, and she is going to tell me that she wants to be back on Earth, back on the beach I've found her on.

Please... no...?

She comes closer to me and pats my chest. I suck in a deep breath, trying my best to not look desperate. "You know, I would have been enjoying the sun, the wind, and the sand. But I ended up spending days on a boring spaceship."

I... At least I entertained her with my cock and she enjoyed that. I'm not going to argue how space travels are often boring anyway. With her, it can be a lot more fun, but... "So... You mean..."

"I want a vacation somewhere."

"Yes, a vacation. Where do you want it to be? A beach? A mountain cottage? A trip to exotic terrains? Check out the mineral mines? Learn to fly a spaceship? Go shop for the newest edition of jewelry?"

"Shop for jewelry?" She laughs. "Which part of me looks like I'd enjoy shopping?"

"Um... Being a female?"

"I'd rather have the food here. I bet your planet has good food, yes?"

I smile. I know from the moment I saw her. She likes good food, and we are going to have a lot of fun together trying out places.

She wraps her arms around her body, even though she isn't hiding much from my eyes. "Hey, what are you looking at?"

I blink and shrug. "Nothing? I'm just thinking about where we can go for good food. You seem to be hiding something from me."

"Oh..." She puts her arms back to her side as if she is trying to hide the fact that she was trying to hide something. "I thought..."

"I'd think you are fat for loving nice food."

"Yeah..." Her cheek is bright red. "I mean—"

"No, I like your curves and I'd like for my mate to eat with me."

"My vacation should come first."

"Will you be my mate if it means all kinds of fun?"

She winks, which makes my heart race again. She doesn't seem as hesitant as before, but a wink isn't a yes, still. "I'll think about it."

Ah! Now, she is being a tease again, and she wants to test how much I will do for her. Fine, I suppose I deserve to have a mate who will demand the best for herself.

"Are you going to pick what you want for the vacation? Or should I pick for you?"

"You said you have things to deliver. Maybe we should do that first. I don't want to cause a delay. Your job and your business are important, too."

I pick her up while she yells and smacks my chest. "I'll make that fun for you. I know you love to be a tease, but when you agree to be my mate, you won't regret it. You won't even think of regretting it."

"Tempting."

She drives me nuts.

And I may like it...

Chapter 13

Galene

I was expecting Vikul to bring me to a boring factory with nothing interesting to do, but this place is beyond my imagination.

He is talking to another being in a language I don't understand. I'm standing in front of a piece of glass that separates out the mining area outside.

It is a large rocky mountain and the factory we are in is at the bottom of it. We are in a crack, barely seeing the sky from the space between the two rocky sides.

The mountain is black, but it isn't made of boring rock. There is a glint in the black, and it feels like I'm staring at a mountain made up of diamonds.

There are blue minerals infused in the black mountain and there are bigger blue crystals protruding from the edges. There are digging robots that look like big beetles with horns. As the horns dig into the mountain, sparkling dust flies. There are a few robots that fly like a hummingbird collecting minerals from the digging robots.

It is dark outside; the mountain above has blocked most of the light. There are some bright spots flying and moving. Maybe that's some bugs that will give light, or maybe it is the shred and dust of the minerals, or maybe another type of robot.

I suck in a breath. This place is unreal. It feels like I'm dreaming. This looks like I'm in one of the fantasy books, inside an enchanted forest. Staring at the shiny and glittering blue and black is almost hypnotic. I can stand here and look at it for the whole day.

A pair of arms wrap around me with a hot and huge body pressing against me. I look up to find Vikul's handsome face.

He rubs my stomach. The other being is probably gone, so he thinks he can do whatever. "Sorry for making you wait."

I squeeze his hand on me. "This place is beautiful."

He grins. "I'm glad you like it. This is a new project. We are excavating a new place."

"It looks like the blue mineral you are going after is going to sell for a lot. It is beautiful."

"Don't you grow to love them?"

The robots are still digging. When the drills hit the rock, there is dust that shines in the air. Doesn't seem to be good to get out there, but it is breathtaking to watch.

"I think I do. It takes time to get into the groove and when it happens, everything is going to click."

He takes in a breath. "And sometimes, things happen at the right times."

"Mmmhmm..."

"There is a part of this site where we developed into a tourist attraction. You are going to enjoy it. We can ride a boat and check out the rocks."

I take a breath, taking in his scent. He warms me with his existence, something I've never felt before. "Every day, you will be here talking to beings. And somehow, you speak my language."

"I do. I trade with humans, so I learn human languages. Not all of them, but the common ones."

"That prepared you well."

"To meet you, yes."

In the window, there is his reflection. The robots are still going, but all I can see is him. His mouth opens and closes as if he has something to say, but figured that he shouldn't.

Silence lingers between us, but it is a comfortable one. I'm here with him, in the mining site, alone.

Maybe he is also watching the robots and the sparkling dust, which are hypnotic and make it easy to keep staring.

"We will be here at times, explore new sites at times, and talk to other beings at times. We can get a lot of time for ourselves. Only the two of us, on the spaceship."

"For you to pin me down and do whatever you want? All the time?"

His cock twitches, and when we are standing with our bodies stuck together, I can feel everything.

He clears his throat. "That will make the trips a lot more interesting. I hope that will be a life you can grow to like."

And be his mate.

That's probably what he has been thinking about and wanting to ask, but he doesn't want to rush me or make things uncomfortable.

I lean into him. "I don't know. It feels scary when I will be here with nothing familiar."

"Because I'm not a human."

"It's not about that. I think I can get used to your purple ass. But… I don't know. We are so far away from Earth and it is scary for me. I don't go traveling a lot and now I'm far away from everything I know."

And… I'm a human, not even a good-looking one. He won't look good with me around. I know nothing about his business and nothing about these planets. I don't even know the language. I'm so dumb and so unhelpful to anything.

He says nothing but holds me even closer. Maybe he worries that I'll want to be back. I think I kind of want to, but it seems like fun to be here with him.

My heart throbs with heat and I can feel the faint but growing bond between him and me again. "What if… I don't fit in?"

"Fit in what? I definitely fit into you."

I smack his hand. He has to get us off track, huh?

"The others on this planet and the different cultures, dammit!"

"I know you will fit in perfectly. Between you and me, we are fine. You are going to do amazing here. Maybe everything is new, but we can learn together. I still owe you a vacation and…"

I turn around and hug him, burying my face in his chest. "You are going to be there with me."

"Yes, if that's what you want. I love every part of you. I don't care what others think about you. You are perfect the way you are."

"But..."

He lifts me off the floor, holding me even tighter. "Please? No buts."

"Are you sure about that? What if I don't look smart--"

He kisses me, stealing my breath and shutting me up. His hot lips burn me and I love the burn. I can feel us, every part of us.

"Galene, you are smart. You are my mate. Let me love you and let me take care of you. Be my mate."

I take a breath. Here goes nothing. "Yes, I will. Vikul, you better behave."

He lets out a low growl and wraps me into his arms again.

"Oof! Vikul!"

"What?" He grunts, holding even tighter. He seemingly has forgotten how I'm a lot smaller than him and he is a bit too strong.

He is holding me so tightly that I almost can't breathe. "My mate."

"Vikul! I'm a human. You're squashing me."

"Oh, sorry!" He puts me down and watches me up close, as if he is worried about me. He should have worried before he attempted to destroy me. "Are you fine? In pain?"

I shake my head. "Maybe feeling silly about getting crushed by a large purple alien."

He chuckles. "I love you."

He hugs me again. This time, he is a lot more careful, almost too careful. I wrap him in my arms, though I still can't wrap him up completely with my short arms.

"Maybe I'm not that strong. I'm not that fragile either."

"Ah, I know." He hugs me back. "You sure can take me well with that tight pussy."

My cheek burns and I peek to see whether there are others here in the corridor. No one is around, but someone can be nearby. What if they heard him?

He chuckles. "It's okay. Even if someone hears us, they won't understand."

"So, you are famous for being horny beyond control?"

He grunts. "You are going to regret that. Now, you aren't going anywhere."

I roll my eyes as I smack his chest again. "Just a horny male, confirmed— Hey!"

He picks me up with his arms under me. "Horny, huh? You are going to regret saying that. If you think that I'm a horny male, I'm going to do just that."

I kick while I laugh. That's what he has been wanting. His excuses won't fly through the radar. "Really? Where're we going?"

"My office. I'm going to make you regret it."

"Regret what? Agreeing to be your mate?"

"Fuck!" He hisses and I love how pissed he is. "I hope not."

"It will depend on what you have for me."

He takes even bigger strides, hurrying to his office, a place where he can take me without worrying about other beings.

I reach for his cock. He is so hard that it may be hard for him to walk.

What have I signed up for again?

He grunts. "Stop being a tease."

"You love me a bit too much anyway."

"Yes, I do. I hate how I do."

"Ah, poor you. There's no escaping now."

"Galene..."

"What?"

"I love you."

"The feeling is very mutual."

Maybe I still have to figure out what I've signed up for, but I know I won't regret it. The heat and the throbbing warmth in my chest grow, seemingly joining my heartbeat with his.

I will never regret this.

Epilogue

Galene

My heart races as the music starts and all the beings in the center of the ballroom start dancing. Vikul wraps an arm around me. "When you feel comfortable, we can also dance."

I shake my head. I hate dancing and when there are that many beings around, hell no.

I take in another breath, letting the luxurious fabric of the purple dress on me settle. The dress is smooth with detailed patterns. Vikul said it shows off my curves perfectly. I don't know about that.

He is in a full suit. But instead of the ones humans wear, he doesn't wear a shirt under the coat. He is in a black and slick cloth with collars, but it looks like a T-shirt more than a shirt, with no buttons. He has a necklace, though. The chain is golden, but it isn't shiny gold, probably another kind of metal. There is a blue mineral as the pedant with marks that are like the ones on his body.

He is handsome and a very good-looking trocul in those clothes. Maybe his confidence is showing off and lifting him.

I still don't understand how I fit in this ballroom. There are statues of unknown creatures at the door and along the walls. Those look like a lion but without the mane. They have sharp and long fangs, but not saber-tooth tigers. The statues have more than two big canines. They have two tails. There are patterns on the bodies, which are unique to each creature. Maybe those are decorative and not exactly how the creatures look, or are imagined.

The walls are black with silver glitters, which kind of look like the ones in Vikul's place, but... There are paintings on the ceiling of beings at a war against some creatures I can't name.

This place looks a bit too luxurious and huge for me to be comfortable.

I pull my eyes from the display and decoration in the room to the long table with food. Not all beings are dancing, some are at the long table taking their share of food, some are chatting by the bar, and some are standing to the side with drinks in their hands.

There are no humans in sight, which...

"Galene..."

"Oh, yes? Sorry, what did I miss?"

Vikul rubs my side. "Getting nervous?"

I nod to a group of five on the other side of the ballroom. I don't even know what species those are. Some have tails, some have horns. "You should be talking to those beings. That's why we are here, right?"

He lets out a soft chuckle. "It is okay. Business can wait. I want you to feel better."

"That's what I want to, but it feels like I'm the only human here and... Almost everyone here is bigger than me and they all look like they know what they are doing here."

"You are here to be a guest, like me. And you are here to enjoy yourself."

"You said this is a business party."

"Party is the key. All beings can use an excuse to enjoy themselves."

He nudges me to go with him, but I have just started to get comfortable standing by the wall and away from everyone else.

I follow him, trying my best to not get tripped up by my dress and heels. I've practiced walking in them, so it should be fine, but I still worry about that all the time.

"Hello!"

I jump when someone talks behind us. I turn around to find a huge male behind us with two curved horns on his head. He has golden scales and a wide grin.

He chuckles. "Hope I didn't scare you. I'm Klouzo. Hope you are enjoying yourself at this party!" He shakes our hands with a bit too much energy in him.

Vikul gives Klouzo a nod. "Nice to meet you. You must be busy."

Klouzo has a bright smile on his face. "Not at all, as long as everyone is happy. Don't remember you having a plus-one last time around."

My heart skips a beat. I suppose there's no reason he can't see my existence, but I hoped he wouldn't make a remark.

Vikul gestures at me. "This is Galene, my mate."

Klouzo gives me a nod. "Nice! I think you should meet Ruby. She is also a human. Seeing how rare you guys are, maybe it will help with the nerves."

I resist the urge to tell Klouzo I'm fine when I'm not, but I don't want to be rude.

Klouzo puts his hand next to his mouth, getting ready to shout when he stops and blinks. "I think I shouldn't shout her name across the room. Give me a second." He hurries off without saying another word and we remain staring at his back.

Vikul chuckles. "Ah, Klouzo is still doing his Klouzo thing."

"What does that mean?"

"Well, he loves parties and everything fun. He is the organizer of this party, getting busy greeting everyone. And he is pretty famous for not following any rules but in a good and creative sense."

"Ah..."

"His mate is also a human, like he mentioned, Ruby."

A woman with wavy hair and a beautiful dress is coming to us, following Klouzo. Klouzo is walking with a bounce in his steps, which doesn't match up perfectly with the suit he is in. He has a bit too much energy for such a formal suit.

She comes over and gives us a nod. "Nice you meet you, Vikul. Hope business is treating you well."

Vikul shakes hand with her. "Thank you for organizing this event. This must be challenging."

"It is worth it." Ruby looks at me. "Hello, nice to meet you. I'm Ruby. I'm Klouzo's... Klouzo... Where are you looking at?"

I turn to follow where Ruby looks, which is also where Klouzo is looking at. A server is walking by with a plate of roasted meat, which smells perfect.

Klouzo clears his throat. "I'm monitoring the quality of food provided for the guests. What did I miss?"

Ruby lets out a soft chuckle, giving Klouzo's hand a squeeze. "Nothing much. This is my mate, Klouzo, if you don't already know. He is focused on..."

Klouzo is watching another plate of cake going through the ballroom by now.

"... Well, making sure everything is working well. We organize events, so he is doing a great job at that. Hope you are having fun here."

I nod. Klouzo doesn't look that scary and Ruby looks nice. "I'm having fun. Will be sure to check out the food soon."

Ruby nods to the long table with freshly made food added almost all the time. The evening is still young, a lot of beings are still waiting to get to their food. "It is a good chance to try out different food from different cultures for sure." She nudges Klouzo. "Let us know if you need anything. We have a few more guests to greet. I look forward to chatting with you later."

Klouzo nods his goodbye. He is still looking for the servers as they walk away.

Vikul lets out a soft sigh. "Well, now you've met the two of them. They were commissioned to host this party for Klouzo's father's company. You bet that male would be rolling his eyes if he saw Klouzo acting like this."

"The father is an uptight business male?"

"Indeed. But Klouzo is so perfect in making everything fun, so organizing parties is perfect for him."

I let out a breath. Klouzo has a way to make me feel a bit more comfortable. He makes the party feel less formal and less tense.

Vikul pulls me to his side, even closer than before. "Are you ready to dance?"

"Um... No...? Do you want to dance?"

If he really wants to, we can. Otherwise, I have no intention of joining the elegantly dancing beings. I'm not that way, and I can't dance without stepping onto Vikul's feet, which I doubt he will enjoy, either.

His eyes darken on me. "If you don't want to dance, I think you owe me some entertainment."

I wriggle my toes with a tinkle going down my spine. From that look, I know what he has in mind and that's lighting a fire in me. "What entertainment?"

"We can get some air on the balcony and get a view of the city."

And probably something else that he isn't telling me at this moment.

"Just like that? Going for some sightseeing?"

He narrows his eyes on me. "Are you going with me?"

I lean closer to him. This is one of the moments when I hate how tall he is. He leans closer to me so I can whisper in his ear. "Are you getting hard? So hard that you have to hide that and can't even stay here in the ballroom."

His grip on my hand tightens, and he groans, softly. "If I wasn't, you'd have tempted me. Go with me, please."

"Ah, with the please, I guess I can't refuse."

"You drive me crazy."

"Glad to be at your service."

He squeezes my hand again, nudging us to get to the side door.

I guess there's no stopping him, which I'm not planning to do anyway.

The balcony is nice with a comforting breeze in the evening. I take a breath, leaning on the railings. The city is beyond us. This hotel is the tallest building among the nearby ones, so it makes for a magnificent view here.

A lot of the lights are still on, painting the city orange and yellow.

"This is nice." I turn to Vikul, who shudders. "You aren't looking at the city."

He swallows, and his gaze darts to the side. "Well, I..."

I reach for his cock. "Already hard now. You just want to get us alone. Fresh air isn't even in the consideration."

He groans and gently pushes my shoulders, turning me around and putting me on the railings. "You can have fun watching the city. I don't mind. We can all use the fresh air."

That is what he said, but he lifts my dress and shoves his hand between my legs.

"Mmm..."

He nibbles on the back of my neck. "Focus on the city."

As he rubs his tip against my entrance? Really?"

I roll my eyes but hold on to the railings with my legs parting for him. "You are no help. What if others see us?"

I shiver at what I said. That is going to be... embarrassing, at least.

He pushes my panties to the side and thrust his thick cock into me, letting his ridges rub my wall. He grunts as he gets deeper and deeper into me, stretching my pussy with his huge cock. "Don't think about anything else."

I shudder when he hit my spot again. He makes that seem easy and makes my pussy contract like a little slut. His cock seems to be angled just right to keep slamming at me.

"Vikul…" I grit my teeth, resisting the urge to moan and scream.

He grabs my waist, slamming in those long, hard strokes as if he is making me every ridge and every scale of his cock. "You are so tight. Fuck…"

I gasp when I hold my breath, taking in the pleasure he sets off. "You have no care about everything else."

"What? You are going to be embarrassed when they come in and see my cock buried deep in you?"

I shiver at his words. He loves to be a tease. My pussy squeezes even tighter around his cock, letting him hit me harder. "Fuck… They are going to think that you are bullying me."

"Why?" His cock twitches and seems to get even hotter.

"Because you are slamming your huge purple cock into me and, fuck, you are such a large purple male."

"I don't see an issue if I keep making you come."

I clench tightly on the railing, so much so I probably can break the marble. I lean onto the railing with my ass in the air. He is holding me, thrusting in so hard that my feet are off the floor. "You love to mess with me."

"Here for the fresh air."

The more he said it, the stronger shame burns in me. I'm out here in the most expensive hotel in the city, on a planet far away from Earth, having my pussy pounded by a huge alien. Fuck...!

My body shudders as I come on his huge cock again.

He kisses the back of my neck, picking up speed. If the railing is any shorter, I may end up falling off the balcony. "I love you. You are so perfect for me. My mate, forever."

A soft moan escapes me when he pulses his hot cum into me. "Vikul... you are so annoying."

"Because I can make you come like no one else can?" He grunts and his hot breath teases me.

"You are horny beyond repair."

"I can fix your wet pussy, though."

I would have smacked his chest if I can, but...

There are footsteps behind us. Maybe someone else is heading here. He groans and helps me to stand on the floor again as he hurries to hide his cock. At least it is easier for me when the dress will hide everything and I can only hope my wetness isn't showing.

We stand side by side at the railings, pretending to be over watching the city.

The heavy frosted glass door opens with a faint hiss and a gust of air. It is soon closed again, probably whoever coming wants their alone time.

When we are alone again, I let go of the railing, also letting out a breath.

Vikul laughs. "I bet they are looking for fresh air, too."

I roll my eyes. "Maybe the actual fresh air."

He clears his throat and fixes his necklace. "We are here for the actual fresh air, too. Didn't you get a lot of that?"

I huff. "I'd get a lot of your cum instead."

"Better than fresh air."

I can't with him... Warmth swirls inside me and I hate to admit how much I enjoy him, like always. He has a big enough ego already.

He snakes his arm around me, pecking a kiss on my forehead. "You still look perfect."

"You still look purple and horny."

He groans with a grin. "Good, then I get to do something more later."

"You still want more?"

He kisses me and it lights another flame in my stomach. "I've warned you. I'm always going to want you."

I let out a soft breath. "Guess it is lucky that I also kind of want you."

He scowls. "Kind of?"

"Yeah, kind of." I wink at him and head to the door leading back to the ballroom. "You better behave, otherwise..."

He murmurs something while he follows. Maybe I can't wait to see what is going to happen after the party. Maybe.

Get a bonus story!

https://icepawpress.com/alina-riley

He doesn't even know what's an Easter Bunny but he hates my event before I can even host it...

This grumpy and annoying grey alien with a tail hates me the moment I show up at the doorstep of the community center. For him, any celebration is stupid. Except I'm going to host the party for the kids and I'm going to do it amazingly well. He won't get to stand in my way. Everything is going great until... my partner for the event falls sick... Now, I need someone to help me with the bunny costume...

Also By Alina Riley

A Mate For The Luraella Traders
Saved by The Alien Boss
Guarded by The Alien Boss
Rescued by The Alien Boss
The Alien Boss's Hook Up

Crashing into an Alien Tribe
Trapped by Snow
Caught by Fire
Stranded by Vine

Mated to the Baekex Bandit
Taken by The Alien Bandit
Saved by the Alien Bandit
Healing the Alien Bandit

Mated to the Zalcor Rebels
The Space Outlaw's Treasure

Also From Ice Paw Press

Dark and Steamy Paranormal Romance

The Wolf's Captive: Collateral

Urban Fantasy

The Hidden Order of Magic: Shaken

The Magic Rebel

Steamy Sci-Fi Romance

A Mate For The Luraella Traders

Crashing into an Alien Tribe

Mated to the Baekex Bandit

Dark Mafia Romance

Kneel to the Jarockis

www.ingramcontent.com/pod-product-compliance
Lightning Source LLC
Chambersburg PA
CBHW031216160726
47992CB00006B/2757